READING CHAMPION

Pip the Different Penguin

by A. H. Benjamin and Bruno Robert

W
FRANKLIN WATTS
LONDON•SYDNEY

"Hello," said a penguin. "I'm Pip."

The other penguins looked at him.

"You look different," they said.

Pip had enormous wings.

"Your wings are silly!"

said the other penguins,

and they walked away.

"But I'm still a penguin,

even if my wings are enormous,"

thought Pip.

3

Later, Pip saw the other penguins

diving into the water.

"It's lunchtime!" they shouted.

Pip wanted to help, but his enormous wings

scared the fish away.

"Go away!" hissed the other penguins.

"We don't need your help!"

5

That afternoon, Pip saw some penguins

on their way to the sea.

They had left their chicks on the ice.

"I can look after the chicks for you," said Pip.

"Please, let me. I'd love to look after them."

"No!" said the chicks' mum and dad.

"You will frighten them

with your enormous wings."

Pip was very upset.

Then the snow came.

The penguins liked to slide down the hill

on their tummies.

"Whee!" they whizzed.

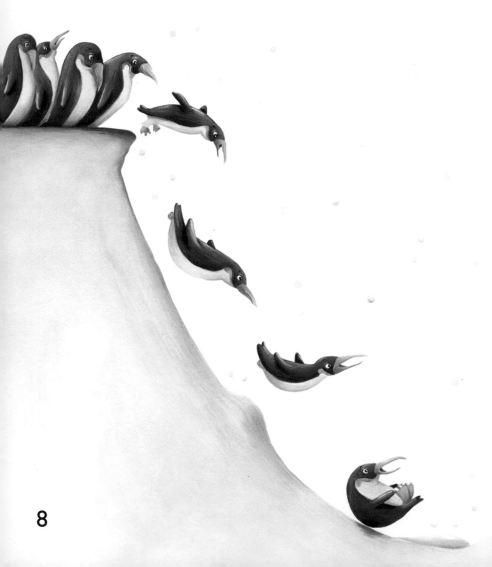

"That looks fun," thought Pip.

He tried to slide down the hill,

but he tripped over his wings and crashed.

"Ha ha!" laughed the other penguins.

"You're so clumsy!"

Poor Pip turned bright red.

The next day, there was a big snow storm.

All the other penguins huddled close together

to keep warm.

Pip wanted to join them,

but they pushed him away.

"Please," said Pip.

"I'm a penguin like you."

"No you are not like us!" said the others.

"You're different. Go away!"

Pip walked away sadly. He went to find a quiet place high on a cliff and sat down. It got colder and colder, but Pip stayed on his spot.

One day, Pip felt the warm sun on his back.

He looked down and saw the other penguins

in the sea. They were having fun.

"Spring has come at last," Pip said to himself.

Just then, he saw a shape swimming
towards the penguins. It was a seal.
"Seals eat penguins!" cried Pip.
"I must tell them!"

But as Pip ran to help, he tripped over

one of his wings and fell off the cliff.

Pip began to flap his wings.

Flap! Flap! he went. Faster and faster.

Harder and harder.

Suddenly, Pip was not falling.

He was flying!

The other penguins saw Pip.

"Look! He can fly!" they gasped.

Pip flew towards the seal,

flapping his enormous wings

and squawking loudly.

The seal was terrified.

It had never seen a penguin fly before.

It dived under the water and swam away.

The other penguins cheered.

"You saved us!" they said. "Thank you!"

An old penguin pushed his way

to the front and everyone stopped to listen.

"Do you know," he said,

"I think we've been unkind to you, Pip.

After all, we're not the same.

Look at me. I have a fat tummy!"

"I have small feet!" said a little penguin.

"My beak is crooked!"

added another penguin.

One by one, the penguins found something

different about themselves.

They all laughed.

"We are all different," said Pip.

"But we are all penguins!"

19

Story order

Look at these 5 pictures and captions.
Put the pictures in the right order
to retell the story.

1

The other penguins made fun of Pip.

2

The penguins said they were all different.

Pip's wings helped him scare off the seal.

The other penguins made Pip feel sad.

Pip went off on his own.

Independent Reading

This series is designed to provide an opportunity for your child to read on their own. These notes are written for you to help your child choose a book and to read it independently.

In school, your child's teacher will often be using reading books which have been banded to support the process of learning to read. Use the book band colour your child is reading in school to help you make a good choice. *Pip the Different Penguin* is a good choice for children reading at Gold Band in their classroom to read independently.

The aim of independent reading is to read this book with ease, so that your child enjoys the story and relates it to their own experiences.

About the book

Pip the penguin has enormous wings. The other penguins in the colony chase Pip away because of them. But when a seal threatens the other penguins, Pip's wings save the day,

Before reading

Help your child to learn how to make good choices by asking:
"Why did you choose this book? Why do you think you will enjoy it?"
Look at the cover together and ask: "What do you think the story will be about?" Ask your child to think of what they already know about penguins. Ask: "What do you think looks different about Pip?" Remind your child that they can sound out the letters to make a word if they get stuck.

Decide together whether your child will read the story independently or read it aloud to you.

During reading

Remind your child of what they know and what they can do independently. If reading aloud, support your child if they hesitate or ask for help by telling the word. If reading to themselves, remind your child that they can come and ask for your help if stuck.

After reading

Support comprehension by asking your child to tell you about the story. Use the story order puzzle to encourage your child to retell the story in the right sequence, in their own words. The correct sequence can be found on the next page.

Help your child think about the messages in the book that go beyond the story and ask: "Why do you think the other penguins are horrible to Pip? When you joined a new group, were the other people nice to you?"

Give your child a chance to respond to the story: "What would you do if you were Pip? Would you help the other penguins when they were in danger, even though they had been mean?"

Extending learning

Help your child reflect on the story, by asking: "What do you think the other penguins have learned from Pip? Do you think they would be kinder to someone else who was different?"

In the classroom, your child's teacher may be teaching different kinds of sentences. There are many examples in this book that you could look at with your child, including statements, commands, exclamations and questions. Find these together and point out how the end punctuation can help us decide what kind of sentence it is.

Franklin Watts
First published in Great Britain in 2018
by The Watts Publishing Group

Series Editors: Jackie Hamley and Melanie Palmer
Series Advisors: Dr Sue Bodman and Glen Franklin
Series Designer: Peter Scoulding

A CIP catalogue record for this book is
available from the British Library.

ISBN 978 1 4451 6257 7 (hbk)
ISBN 978 1 4451 6258 4 (pbk)
ISBN 978 1 4451 6256 0 (library ebook)

Printed in China

Franklin Watts
An imprint of
Hachette Children's Group
Part of The Watts Publishing Group
Carmelite House
50 Victoria Embankment
London EC4Y 0DZ

An Hachette UK Company
www.hachette.co.uk

www.franklinwatts.co.uk

Answer to Story order: 4, 1, 5, 3, 2